The Missing Pony Mystery

THE BOBBSEY TWINS®

THE
MISSING PONY
MYSTERY

Laura Lee Hope

Illustrated by Ruth Sanderson

WANDERER BOOKS
Published by
Simon & Schuster, New York

Published by WANDERER BOOKS
A Simon & Schuster Division of
Gulf & Western Corporation
Simon & Schuster Building
1230 Avenue of the Americas
New York, New York 10020

Manufactured in the United States of America
10 9 8 7 6 5 4 3

WANDERER and colophon are trademarks of Simon & Schuster

THE BOBBSEY TWINS, NANCY DREW, and THE HARDY BOYS
are trademarks of Stratemeyer Syndicate, registered in the United
States Patent and Trademark Office

Library of Congress Cataloging in Publication Data

Hope, Laura Lee.
The missing pony mystery.

(The Bobbsey twins; 4)
SUMMARY: The Bobbsey twins try to track down a missing pony and
saddlebag.
    [1.   Mystery and detective stories] I. Sanderson,
Ruth.   II. Title.   III.   Series: Hope, Laura Lee.
    Bobbsey twins (New York, 1980-   ); 4.
    PZ7.H772Mi   [Fic]   80-25802
        ISBN 0-671-42295-2
        ISBN 0-671-42296-0 (pbk.)

Contents

·1·

The Contest

Twelve-year-old Nan Bobbsey listened to her friend Nellie Parks on the telephone. Her dark eyes shone with excitement, and a happy smile spread over her face. After talking for a few minutes, she skipped into the kitchen where Mrs. Bobbsey and Nan's twin brother, Bert, were fixing sandwiches while Freddie and Flossie, the younger twins, made lemonade.

"Mother, Nellie says there's an amateur contest for children on TV channel forty. She thinks our singing group might have a chance to win!"

"Oh, great!" Bert said. He had been taking guitar lessons while Mrs. Bobbsey had taught Nan and the younger children to play the piano.

"How 'citing," Flossie said, and shook her blond curls. "When is the contest going to be?"

"Friday night," Nan replied. "Less than a week to get ready. And there's going to be a prize," she added.

"What is it?" her mother inquired.

"That's a secret. They won't tell."

"Do you have to fill out an application?" Mrs. Bobbsey asked.

"Nellie doesn't know," Nan said. "I'll find out."

After lunch, Bert looked at his wristwatch. "Time to go to the stables," he announced.

The children liked to ride, and often did chores at a nearby stable. On Saturday afternoons, Bert currycombed the horses while Nan took care of the younger children at the pony track. Six-year-old Freddie and Flossie went along to help. Their favorite animal was a Shetland pony named Cupcake.

The youngsters ran outside and piled into the station wagon. With Mrs. Bobbsey at the wheel, they set off for the riding club.

"Mommy, I love Cupcake. He's so *bee-yoo-ti-ful*," Flossie said as she settled herself next to her mother.

"Cupcake's cute," Mrs. Bobbsey admitted. "And those Shetlands love people, too. Did you know that they were work animals for hundreds of years?"

"Where?" Freddie spoke up.

"In Scotland," his mother answered, and explained that the Shetland pony, the smallest of all modern horses, came from the Shetland Islands, north of Scotland. "Its big mop of mane served as a shield for the pony's eyes in the wind and rain," she added, "and its long hair made a good raincoat."

Mrs. Bobbsey turned onto a private road and soon entered the riding club located at the foot of a hill fringed with high grass.

There were two stables, the larger one for horses, the smaller one for ponies. In front of each was a riding ring. Beyond the hill, the ground rose sharply until it met a pinewoods. A bridle trail led from the riding academy south for several miles, continuing into Lakeside State Park.

With a whoop of joy, the Bobbsey twins jumped out of the car. Bert and Freddie hurried into the large stable and went straight to a slender, bushy-bearded man saddling a horse. He wore boots, jodhpurs, and a sweat shirt.

"Hello, Wink! Lots of business today?" Bert asked.

"More people than ever," replied the stable manager. Cobb Winkler, affectionately called Wink by most of the children, loved music. He was Bert's guitar teacher.

The boy went to work quickly. He picked up a currycomb and started to groom a big chestnut mare while Freddie helped Wink put fresh water in the stalls.

Outside, the two girls ran to the pony

stables where Nan found Mr. Rockwell, owner of the riding club. He was a portly man with kind brown eyes.

"Oh, Nan," Mr. Rockwell said, "better get over to the corral right away. Three kids are waiting for pony rides."

Nan hurried into the stables, and with the help of her sister, led three ponies out into the ring. Flossie walked Cupcake, who was the smallest, and Nan trotted between two others named Red and Pepper.

As Nan helped two girls and a boy mount the ponies, Mrs. Bobbsey waved good-bye to them. "I'm going shopping," she called. "Pick you up later."

The girls worked for an hour, but finally there was a lull in the pony-ride business. This gave Nan and Flossie their chance.

"Now we can ride," Nan said. She boosted Flossie atop Cupcake, and the little girl's bright eyes danced.

Nan was mounting Pepper when a boy ran up to the corral gate. He was about Bert's age, but taller and heavier, and wore a permanent scowl. Frowning at Nan, he said loudly, "I want a ride." Nan recognized him immediately as Danny Rugg, the town bully.

She slid off Pepper's back and walked over to the boy. "Do you have your ticket?" she asked.

"Aw, I don't need any ticket," Danny declared. "We're neighbors, aren't we? Can't I get a ride free?"

"We're not neighbors," Nan said. "And you'll have to pay just like anyone else. That's Mr. Rockwell's rule."

"You and your sister get rides free!" Danny challenged.

"We work here," Nan said.

"Oh, you Bobbseys think you're so smart," Danny declared. He sidestepped to where Cupcake and Flossie were waiting patiently. Then, with a quick motion, he slapped the pony hard on the flank.

Startled, Cupcake broke into a trot, throwing the little girl to the ground.

"Flossie, are you all right?" Nan exclaimed and rushed to her sister's aid.

Flossie started to cry. "I'm not hurt, but

look at Cupcake! He's running away!"

"Cupcake, come back!" Nan shouted as the girls hurried after the pony. But the little hooves flashed as the Shetland ran up the slope toward the woods.

Just then the girls saw a man step out from among the trees and dash up to the pony. He grabbed the bridle and led Cupcake into the woods!

·2·

A Diamond Clue

Cupcake was gone. The girls strained their eyes hard to see him, but there was no sign of the pony.

Flossie was in tears. "Oh, Nan, what'll we do?" she cried.

"Tell Bert. Come on. Hurry!" The sisters ran into the horse barn where they found Bert and Freddie raking straw from the stalls.

"Bert, something terrible has happened!" Nan said. "Cupcake's gotten away!"

"Stolen by a bad man!" Flossie added.

"What!"

"Come here, I'll show you!" Nan led the

boys outside and pointed up the hill, at the same time telling what had happened.

"Nan, you stay with Flossie," Bert suggested. "Freddie and I'll try to rescue Cupcake."

As the two boys raced off, Bert whistled to Charlie Mason, a friend his own age, and shouted what had happened.

"I'll help you," Charlie volunteered and dashed after the Bobbsey boys.

When they reached the edge of the woods, Freddie looked back and waved reassuringly to his sisters. Bert quickly found Cupcake's tracks, and the boys followed them into the woods.

"From the looks of the hoof marks," Bert said, "Cupcake was galloping."

"Right," Charlie agreed. "The thief's trying to get him away as quickly as possible."

After ten minutes of searching, Bert pointed. "Look, there's a road." They ran to the side of a very straight blacktop highway that led north and south. They crossed to the other side, but there were no more hoof marks among the trees.

"The thief must have put Cupcake in a truck and carried him off," Bert said. His keen eyes scanned both sides of the highway until they lighted on a tire track.

"Charlie! Freddie! Look at this!" All three bent down to study the mark. Charlie guessed that a vehicle had pulled off to the side, and one tire had left a diamond pattern in the sandy earth.

"Don't touch it," Bert warned. "It may be an important clue."

"What good are clues without Cupcake?" Freddie wailed.

Bert sighed and stood up. "You're right. Well, whoever stole Cupcake made a clean getaway."

"What'll we do now?" Charlie asked.

"Go back and report to Mr. Rockwell," Bert said.

As the three boys retraced their steps through the woods, they talked about the mysterious stranger who had run off with the pony. Why would anyone do such a thing? And why was the man lurking at the edge of the woods at that very moment?

"Maybe he was looking over the stables and getting ready to steal another animal," Bert reasoned.

When they came to the edge of the woods, the boys found Nan and Flossie waiting for them.

"Where's Cupcake?" Flossie asked.

"We didn't find him," Bert replied.

"I told you, Nan," Flossie sniffled. "Cupcake's gone forever. We'll never see him again!"

"Oh, Flossie, don't say that. Of course we'll get him back. Nobody can hide a pony forever!"

Flossie stopped crying, and all the children ran down the hill to the big barn to tell Wink about the missing animal.

"I'm afraid that's bad," Wink said, shaking his head and stroking his beard. "I haven't heard of horse thieves since long ago when I was a boy in Tennessee. You'd better go tell Mr. Rockwell what happened."

The youngsters found the manager hitching Pepper to a pony cart. When he was told of the theft, Mr. Rockwell said, "I'll phone the police immediately." He went to his office which was located at one end of the pony stables.

Bert and Freddie went back to their work in the stable, but their minds were far away with thoughts of Cupcake. The girls returned to the pony corral, looking sad and worried.

Late in the afternoon, Mrs. Bobbsey came to pick up her children. "Gracious, why the long faces?" she commented, and soon learned the reason.

"Oh, that poor little pony," she said. "Don't worry, though. The police will find him."

"I don't know, Mommy," Flossie said. "Maybe that bad man will take him back to Scotland!"

Before saying good-bye to Wink, Bert asked, "How about my guitar lesson next week?"

"Will Monday afternoon be all right?"

"Fine."

After they had driven home, the children helped carry the groceries into the kitchen. Mrs. Bobbsey opened a package of cookies and let the youngsters help themselves, but Flossie wouldn't even nibble on hers.

"Don't be so sad, Floss," her mother said. "Come here." She took the little girl and hugged her. Just then Mr. Bobbsey, who owned a lumberyard in Lakeport, came home from work. The youngsters told their father all that had happened that day.

He was sorry about the missing pony, but agreed with Nan that the police would no doubt find the thief. "Nothing much gets past Chief Smith," he said.

After dinner, the children were playing in the yard when a police car pulled up and the chief climbed out.

"I hear you children witnessed a theft," the officer, who was a good friend of the family, called out.

"That's right," Bert said. "Will you help us catch the bad guy, Chief?"

"Tell you what I'll do. I'm off duty tomorrow afternoon. Suppose we drive to this road and look it over together."

"Great!" Nan declared. Then the chief went into the house to talk to her parents. After he had left, Mrs. Bobbsey called the children inside. "Time for bed," she said. "It's getting late."

Before saying good-night, Nan asked her father, "What song shall we sing for the TV contest, Dad?"

"I'd say it should either be a top favorite or one that few people have heard. The latter may be hard to find. Give me some time to think about—"

He was interrupted by a sudden *bang* on the window. The next instant, a loud explosion shattered the evening stillness!

·3·

Freddie's Idea

"That was a firecracker!" Bert said. He jumped up, dashed outside, and ran around the house. All was quiet, and no one was in sight.

"Who did it, Bert?" Freddie called out.

"A wise guy, I guess."

Just then Nan and Flossie joined the search. Each carried a flashlight.

"Now we can get a better look," Nan said. They made their way to the window beneath which the blast had been set off. Bits of red and gray paper proved that Bert's guess about a firecracker was right. Suddenly, the beam of Flossie's light hit a square piece of paper thumbtacked directly under the sill. Bert pried out the tack, then opened the paper.

"Hold your flashlight closer, Floss," he said, "so I can see."

The note, in scrawled printing, read:

I KNOW WHERE CUPCAKE IS. PUT 20 DOL-LARS IN A PACKAGE AND BURY IT AT THE RIGHT-HAND POST OF THE CORRAL GATE. THEN I WILL TELL YOU.

"Oh, how awful!" cried Nan. "Mother, Dad, look at this!"

Her parents, who had followed the children into the yard, read the message and shook their heads.

"Just a childish trick," Mr. Bobbsey declared. "And the firecracker was meant to get our attention."

"What should we do about it, Daddy?" Flossie asked.

"Ignore it," her father advised. "I'm sure the writer doesn't know where Cupcake is."

"But who would do such a thing?" Nan persisted.

"Maybe Danny Rugg," Freddie said. "He was mean enough to hit Cupcake."

Bert shrugged. "I guess Dad's right. We'll forget it."

"Not me," Freddie piped up. "I'll think of something we can do to get even!"

"Now, Freddie," Mrs. Bobbsey said firmly, "don't talk about getting even."

"Especially," Nan added with a chuckle, "when you don't know whom to get even with!"

"Maybe you're right," Freddie said. He rolled his eyes and ran his fingers through his blond curls. "But I'll think of something."

After church the next day, the Bobbseys strolled home to have midday dinner. Some time later, Chief Smith arrived and the children told him about the firecracker and the ransom note. When Nan showed it to him, he studied the message carefully. Then he said, "This was probably written by a boy who's been watching too many TV mysteries."

"Do you suppose he knows where Cupcake is?" Flossie asked.

"I doubt it. He just wants—"

He was interrupted by a shout from Freddie. "Here comes Danny Rugg!"

The children ran to the front porch and saw the bully walking slowly down the opposite side of the street. He cast an occasional sidelong glance at the Bobbsey home.

"Does he ever look guilty!" Nan said.

"Hey, Firecrackers!" Bert called out. "You want your money now or later?"

Danny whirled about. "What do you mean?"

"You know," Bert said, striding toward him.

Danny stepped back. "I don't want to fight," he whined.

"Who said fight? But tell me, why'd you leave a note at our house?"

"I didn't leave any old note!" Danny muttered.

"All right, we'll see." Bert called Nan to his side. After he whispered to her, the girl went into the house and returned with a pencil and pad of paper. Bert held them out to Danny. "Now let's see you print the alphabet."

"What kind of a nutty trick is this?" The other boy scowled.

Just then Chief Smith stepped outside. When Danny Rugg saw him, his eyes bugged wide. "I'm getting out of here!" he exclaimed, and raced down the street.

"Wow! Did you see him go?" Bert chuckled. "Like a scared rabbit!"

"Do you think he wrote the note?" Nan asked.

"I don't know," Bert admitted.

"Well, let's go and do a little mixing," the chief suggested, and led the way to his car.

"What are we going to mix?" Bert asked.

"Tell you later."

Bert and Nan climbed into the car, but Freddie and Flossie decided to stay home and play. As the chief started the engine, Freddie rode his bike around in circles in the middle of the street. He always did this when he was thinking hard about something.

"Freddie, what's on your mind?" Bert asked through the open window.

"A plan."

"What kind?"

"I don't know yet," Freddie replied.

He wrinkled his nose and kept circling.

On their way to the woods, Chief Smith said, "Bert, can you lead me to the exact spot where Cupcake's tracks disappeared?"

"Yes, I can."

The officer turned onto the highway over which the pony's kidnapper had made his getaway. Soon they were on a straight stretch leading to the state park.

"Slow down, Chief," Bert directed. "We're getting closer." A few moments later he exclaimed, "There's the place!"

The chief pulled to the side of the road and all three got out and looked around. Bert quickly found the tire print. It had not been disturbed.

"Lucky for us it hasn't rained," the officer said and opened the trunk of his car. He took out a container of water, a small bag of white powdery plaster, and a rectangular frame about two feet wide.

Bert snapped his fingers. "I get it! We're going to make a plaster cast of this tire mark!"

"Right," the chief replied. "You can help me with it."

Following instructions, Nan poured the plaster slowly into the water, while Bert stirred with a long stick.

"When it's ready, it should be about as

thick as melted ice cream," Chief Smith said.

"It's that way now," Nan reported.

"All right, bring it over here, then." The chief placed the wooden frame over the print, then went back to the trunk for a push-button can.

"What's that?" Bert asked.

"Plastic spray. Now watch." The officer sprayed over the print and waited for a few minutes. Then he poured the mixture carefully into the mold.

"I want to compare this with another mold made some time ago," he said, while they were waiting for the mix to harden. When it was ready, he picked up the frame and turned it over.

"A perfect print!" Bert called out.

"There's a small chance it'll lead to something," Chief Smith said and carried the impression to the car. "Good detectives must look at every clue."

When they reached the Bobbsey home, Freddie was still riding his bicycle.

"I've got an idea, Bert! A great idea!" the little boy cried out.

"What is it?" Bert asked.

"It's a secret. I won't tell until everyone is together."

The chief smiled. "I'll say good-bye," he said. "And, Bert, I'll let you know whether our clue's a foul ball or a home run."

"Now what's the big deal?" Nan asked as the car left.

"Come down to the basement."

With Freddie in the lead, and Flossie joining them, the children went down the cellar steps. They stopped at a toy box belonging to Flossie. From it, Freddie picked a square carton.

"That's mine," Flossie spoke up.

"I know. Santa Claus brought it." Freddie opened the tiny latch and—*whump!* A rubber frog jumped out and hit the ceiling.

The children stared at it in amazement.

"*That's* my idea!" Freddie shouted.

·4·

A Surprise Catch

"What kind of super idea is that?" Flossie asked.

"Don't you see?" Freddie said. "We can bury the frog instead of the money!"

"You mean, hide it near the corral gate, as the note said?"

"Sure. And when Danny digs it up, zowie!"

"That's not bad," Bert had to admit. "Danny doesn't get his money, but instead gets scared."

Freddie's brown eyes flashed with excitement. "The best part of all," he said, "is that we can catch him!" He returned the frog to its box, pushed down the lid, and locked it.

"Let's bury the frog just before dark," Nan suggested. "Then we'll hide and watch."

When Mrs. Bobbsey heard about their plan, she thought it best that Flossie and Freddie remain at home, and added, "I don't want the rest of you getting into any trouble, do you hear?"

"Oh, we won't," Nan promised.

After dinner, Nan telephoned the TV station to ask about the amateur contest. When she hung up, she said, "One of us will have to go there to get an entry blank."

"Okay," Bert said. "But right now we'd better get to the stable."

The twins hopped on their bikes. Nan carried the jumping frog in a shopping bag on her handlebar. By the time they arrived, the pony corral was already closed, and the last few horses were being led into the stalls by Wink.

The twins parked their bicycles and ran

to tell their friend what had happened.

"Well, I'll be—!" Wink exclaimed when he saw the children. "You didn't come down here to work, did you?"

"Of course not," Nan replied.

"Then you have news about Cupcake?"

"No, not yet," Bert said. "But we've come here on account of Cupcake."

Wink shook his head and hooked his thumbs into his suspenders. "Sounds mighty mysterious to me," he said. "What's up?"

Bert told him about the note they had received the night before and of their plan to fool the person who had written it.

"I see, I see," Wink said. "You're going to scare the wits out of him, and he deserves it!"

"You won't let on we're hiding, will you?" Bert asked.

"Of course not. Matter of fact, I have a good idea for a hiding place."

The youngsters glanced toward the corral gate. There were no bushes near it, and the fence posts were too narrow to conceal anyone.

"I don't see any," Bert said.

"Bury the box first," Wink suggested. "You know where we keep the shovels."

The boy ran to get one, and the Bobbseys walked toward the corral. They glanced about to see if anyone was watching. Nobody was in sight. At the gate, Bert dug a hole in the soft earth.

"Is that big enough?" he asked Nan.

The girl placed the shopping bag in the hole. "Good."

Bert covered the sack lightly with a thin layer of earth, then tamped it down and looked all around once more. The last horseback rider had left, and it was growing dark.

On the way back to the barn, the children saw Wink pulling a pony cart. "Is the box buried?" he asked.

"Yes," Bert said. "Wink, where'll we hide?"

"In here."

"I don't get it," Nan said.

The stable manager rested the shafts on the ground and explained. He would put the twins into the pony cart, cover them with a tarpaulin, and park the cart near the corral gate.

"I leave the carts out sometimes," he said, "so nobody'll think it's unusual."

"That's a great idea!" Bert said.

"You can peek out from under the tarp," Wink went on, "and watch for that rascal in comfort."

"That is, if he comes," Nan said.

"Don't worry, I have a feeling he will," Wink said. "Now ride your bikes down to the entrance and leave them in the tall grass. Circle back around the pony barn and come in the rear door. I'll meet you there."

The children did as they were told. Then, bending low, they made their way to the back of the barn, opened the door carefully, and stepped inside. They found themselves face to face with Wink.

"You see anyone?" he asked.

"No, sir," Bert replied.

"Then follow me!"

The youngsters ran to the pony cart and climbed inside. Wink put a canvas covering over them. "Say, you're a load!" he whispered as he lifted the shafts and pulled the cart away.

The Bobbseys felt a rising excitement as they were trundled along. Soon the cart stopped and they heard the shafts hit the ground.

"Good luck," came Wink's low voice, and the children settled down to wait. All was silent, except for the crickets' chirring and an owl hooting somewhere in the woods.

Five minutes went by, and another five. Nan and Bert peeked from under the tarpaulin into the darkness. A light fog, silvery in the light of the moon, drifted in over the meadow.

"Bert, how long will we have—"

"Shh! I think I see something."

The twins gazed down the lane. A flashlight bobbed this way and that, as if someone were walking toward the corral.

Nan and Bert hardly dared to breathe, and their hearts thumped.

Suddenly the light stood still. "Whoever it is, he's looking around," Bert whispered.

The light advanced again, straight toward the corral gate. Bert saw that the prowler was a boy but could not make out his face.

Now the stranger laid his flashlight on the ground and dropped to his knees, next to the freshly covered hole. He began to dig with both hands, like a dog digging for a bone. The Bobbseys heard the shopping bag rattle.

Suddenly there was a *click*. A howling scream of fright shattered the stillness as the frog jumped out of the box and hit the boy in the face!

Bert threw the tarpaulin off and hurled himself directly at the figure. The two rolled over and over.

Nan joined in the fight, and finally their opponent stopped struggling as Bert sat

astride his chest. The moonlight shone down into the captive's scowling face.

"Danny Rugg!" Bert exclaimed. "We figured it would be you!"

"Where's Cupcake? Is he all right?" Nan demanded, standing up and brushing her clothes.

"I don't know," Danny said defiantly.

"Did you write this ransom note?" Bert prodded.

Silence.

"Answer me!"

"Yes," Danny mumbled. "It was a joke. I was only doing it for fun!"

"But you expected us to leave the money, didn't you?" Nan asked.

"Let me up!" Danny begged.

Bert got off his prisoner's chest, but held him firmly by the collar. Danny was still shaking from fright.

"You're a meanie!" Nan said. "You ought to be ashamed of yourself."

Convinced that Danny knew nothing more about Cupcake, Bert released him.

Danny picked up his flashlight and slunk off into the darkness.

"That should teach him a lesson," Nan said, and the twins pulled the pony cart back to the barn. Wink met them there. When he heard what had happened, the stable manager chuckled. "You must've scared him out of a year's growth!"

The children thanked their friend for his help, then got on their bicycles and sped home.

Their parents were very amused when they heard the story, and the younger twins bent over laughing.

"Danny got it right in the nose!" Freddie exclaimed.

"That'll give him something to dream about," Flossie giggled.

Next morning, Bert was on his way home after running an errand for his mother when a car pulled up beside him. He recognized Chief Smith.

"Oh, hello, Chief," the boy greeted the officer. "We had some fun last night."

Quickly he reported their encounter with Danny Rugg at the corral gate.

"Good work!" the chief complimented him with a grin. "And now I have some good news for you, too. You've hit a home run!"

·5·

More Trouble

At first Bert was puzzled. "A home run?" he asked, and then the meaning dawned on him. "Oh, the tire tracks!"

"Right. You found a terrific clue!" Chief Smith said that the model they had made the day before matched exactly another tread mark discovered several weeks ago.

"We found the other print near the riding academy in Chatham where two valuable horses were stolen," the officer added.

"I remember reading about that," Bert said. "The thief got away, didn't he?"

"Yes, and the only clue was the diamond tire track we found near the scene."

Bert looked jubilant. "Maybe the same man who stole the two horses kidnapped Cupcake."

The officer nodded. "Apparently the thief is familiar with this area; he may even live around here."

Just then they heard the radio squawk. The chief excused himself and drove off.

Later that day, Bert slung his guitar over his back. "Nan, you want to come along to the stables?" he asked his sister.

"Yes, wait for me."

When the two reached the riding club, Nan picked a gray horse named Dusk and saddled up while Bert found his friend Wink at the horse barn.

"Here I am for my lesson," the boy said.

"Okay, you play your guitar while I work," the stable manager replied. Bert twanged the strings and struck up a tune he had just learned. Wink checked frequently to see that his fingering was correct.

"Good! You're doing well," Wink said. "Now play those last two bars again."

When Bert finished his lesson, he told

Wink about the TV amateur contest.

"I know just what you need to win," Wink said, snapping his suspenders. "How about an old Tennessee ballad about a pony?"

"That sounds great!" Bert exclaimed. "Do you have the music?"

The man stroked his beard thoughtfully and replied, "I did have a copy, but it disappeared." He said he had kept the piece in an old saddlebag in the room he occupied at the rear of the pony stable.

"The bag's clean gone! Just got up and walked away, I guess."

"That can't be," Bert declared. "Somebody must have taken it."

"But who'd want an old saddlebag?" the man asked.

"Somebody could've been prowling around, looking for a chance to take things," the boy reasoned.

Wink shrugged. "Maybe I mislaid it," he said. "Who can tell?" He went off to feed another horse.

His lesson over, Bert sat in front of the

stable, picking away at the guitar. All the while he thought about the disappearance of the saddlebag and the old Tennessee ballad.

Finally, Nan returned from her ride, sitting tall on Dusk's back, holding the reins lightly. She dismounted and led the horse inside.

"Good girl," she said, patting the mare's nose. "That was a nice ride."

Dusk bobbed her head and nickered. Nan loosened the cinch straps, removed the saddle and bridle, then walked the mare into her stall.

The girl was about to join Bert when suddenly she saw a man at the far end of the barn. He wore slacks, a sports jacket, and a plaid hat pulled low over his face. The stranger was lifting a sack of oats off the floor.

"Hello," Nan called out. "Are you helping Wink?"

Caught by surprise, the fellow hunched his shoulders and bent his head lower. With a mighty tug, he lifted the sack on his back, strode forward, and pushed roughly past Nan.

"Get out of my way!" he growled.

"Stop!" Nan cried. "You can't take that! It doesn't belong to you."

The man paid no attention as he hurried out the door with the sack of oats.

Nan's first thought was to mount Dusk and ride after the thief. But she had already unsaddled, and it was too difficult to ride bareback.

She glanced out of the door to see the fellow scurrying toward the woods. "Help! Help!" she screamed.

Bert rushed to her side, followed by Wink.

"That man's stealing your oats!" Nan cried.

"Come on! After him!" Bert ordered. He put his guitar beside the stable wall, and the two children sprinted across the flat stretch behind the barn, then up the slope to the woods.

"We're gaining on him!" Bert shouted.

Hearing the young voice, the man hesitated and looked back. Realizing he could never escape with such a heavy load, he ripped the bag open and poured half the contents on the ground. The oats fell over his shoes and pants. Then he swung the sack back onto his shoulder and began to run again.

No use. The Bobbseys were too fast. He dropped the sack and hurried into the woods.

"He's heading for the road!" Bert shouted as they dashed among the pine trees. Suddenly a small gully loomed ahead. It was partly filled with rainwater.

Splash! The man plowed through, knee-deep. Bert and Nan followed. As the thief scrambled up the muddy slope, he slid backward. Bert grabbed his jacket, but the fellow wrenched free and kicked. His foot hit Bert in the chest, and the boy fell, knocking Nan off her feet at the same time!

·6·

Futile Chase

"Catch him! Catch him!" Nan cried frantically as she scrambled to her feet. The twins struggled up the muddy slope, but the man was far ahead of them, nearly at the road.

Bert and Nan were still running when they heard the sound of a motor. As they reached the pavement, they saw a dark green delivery truck streaking off in the direction of the state park.

"There he goes!" Nan said. "Oh, if there were only some way to catch him!"

"I'd like to get my hands on him!" Bert said hotly. "I bet he's the one who stole Cupcake!"

"Sure. That's why he took the oats, but I spoiled his plans," Nan said. "I almost wish I hadn't seen him. Now poor Cupcake will go hungry!"

"Let's look for tire prints," Bert suggested. "The ground's still damp. We might find some good ones."

They separated, each examining one side of the road. Finally Nan called out, "Bert, I found some!"

Her brother hurried to her side, and gasped. "Wow! The diamond pattern!"

"Then we were right," Nan said. "That was the truck that carried Cupcake away!"

Excited with their discovery, the children hurried back through the woods. On the way, they met Wink, who had picked up the sack of oats.

"What happened?" he asked.

The children told their story and the stableman's mouth dropped open. "Well, I'll be—!" he said in amazement. "You nearly did get him!"

"Almost," Bert said in disgust. When

they returned to the stables, he called the police. Chief Smith was not at headquarters, so the boy left a message, describing the getaway truck.

Half an hour later the twins went home, muddy and damp.

"Goodness!" Mrs. Bobbsey exclaimed. "Did you fall off a horse?"

While the younger twins listened wide-eyed, Bert and Nan told about their adventure. Hearing about the oats, Flossie began to cry. "Poor Cupcake," she said. "He'll get thinner and thinner until he's just bones in a fur coat."

"Don't worry," Bert assured her. "We'll find Cupcake in time. That thief can't hide his green truck much longer."

"That's right," Nan added. "Not with the police looking for him."

"Now off to the bathroom," Mrs. Bobbsey said. "You both need a shower and a change of clothes."

Before suppertime, the Bobbseys got a call from Chief Smith. He thanked them for the new information and said both the police and the State Motor Vehicle Bureau were working on the case.

"I'm sure that crook is hiding out somewhere in the woods," Bert said to Freddie after he hung up. "Probably somewhere between here and the state park."

Freddie nodded. "Maybe we should search the pinewoods for him."

"How about a camping trip?" Bert suggested. "We'll ask Charlie Mason to come with us."

"Good idea!" Freddie agreed. "Let's call Charlie."

Their friend was eager for the adventure, and both Charlie's parents and Mr. and Mrs. Bobbsey permitted the boys to go on an overnight trip.

"You mean, the girls aren't included?" Nan asked, her chin up in the air. "Well, in that case, we'll do something special by ourselves."

"What do you mean?" Freddie asked.

Nan just smiled and went to the telephone. She called Nellie Parks, and when her friend answered, she put a hand around the mouthpiece and lowered her voice.

When the conversation was over, Freddie asked, "What are you up to, Nan?"

"We're going to be detectives."

"You and Nellie?"

Nan nodded. "And what we're going to do is our secret!"

Next morning, Nan spoke to her mother. "I'm going to visit Nellie. May I take Flossie with me?"

"Of course, if she wants to go along."

Nan found Flossie in their room. "Floss, I have some detective work to do. Would you like to help me?"

"About Cupcake?"

When Nan nodded, Flossie smiled. "Sure, I'll help you," she said. Hand in hand, the sisters walked to Nellie's home. Halfway there, they met Danny riding his bicycle.

"Pay no attention to him," Nan said, looking straight ahead.

The boy rode along the curb beside them. "You still trying to find Cupcake?" he asked with a laugh.

Nan and Flossie did not reply but quickened their step.

"You'll never find him," continued the boy as he pedaled along. "By now they've made glue out of that old pony!"

·7·
Bubbles

Flossie started to cry. "Oh, Nan, wouldn't that be terrible if they really made glue out of Cupcake?"

"Don't believe it!" Nan said and squeezed her sister's hand tightly. "Danny's only trying to make us nervous, that's all."

The two girls met Nellie skipping rope in front of her house. "Hi," she said brightly. "Are you ready to start now?"

"Yes," Nan replied. "Let's begin with Gruber's."

The trio went downtown and walked into

Gruber's Dry Cleaning Shop. The owner was hanging freshly pressed suits on a pipe rack.

"Mr. Gruber," Nan said, "has anybody brought in some real muddy pants with oats in the cuffs?"

"What about goats?"

Nan laughed. "Not goats. Oats. You know, what they feed horses."

"Oh, no," Mr. Gruber replied. He looked curiously at the girls. "Why would anybody have oats in the cuffs of his pants?"

Briefly Nan told him about the pony thief.

"Oh, I see," the man said. "Well, there are a lot of people in Lakeport, and lots of cleaning places. I'm afraid you'll have to try them all. Wait here a moment."

The cleaner disappeared into the back of his shop and returned a minute later with a short list in his hand. "Here are all the addresses," he said. "Good luck!"

"Thank you," Nan said, taking the list. She looked it over quickly.

"Let's go to De Luxe Cleaners next," she said to Flossie and Nellie. "It's only two blocks down the street."

When they entered the store, Flossie blurted out quickly, "Do you have any cuffs with oats in them?"

The woman behind the counter looked surprised. "Cuffs with oats in them? Do you feel all right, little girl?"

Nan explained more clearly. When she had finished, the clerk raised her eyebrows. "A man with really muddy pants?" she said. "Yes! Early this morning, a fellow brought a pair in."

"Did he give his name?" Nellie asked.

"No, I wouldn't take his pants. They were too muddy. I told him if he washed them first, we would press them for him. I even suggested a laundromat down the street."

"Did he go there?" Flossie asked.

"I think so."

After thanking the woman, the three girls hurried from the shop toward the laundromat. As they did, a voice called out, "Nan! Wait for me!"

The girls whirled about to see Freddie trotting toward them.

"I want to be in on the fun," the little boy said. "I want to be a detective too."

"All right," Nan said. She told her brother what they were looking for.

He nodded approvingly. "I get it. If you find the pants, you find the man. Not bad."

The children entered the laundromat and looked around. Several customers were in the place, but Freddie hardly noticed them. His big eyes danced with joy as he took in the bright interior. A double row of washing machines ran the length of the store—two dozen in all. Opposite them were the dryers with their big glass doors. An empty clothes carrier was parked against one of them. Freddie lifted his sister and she climbed into it.

"This is great," he said, as he pushed his sister around the laundromat.

Nan and Nellie, however, had more serious matters in mind. Of all the customers,

only two were men. Nan realized that nei-
ther looked like the thief. But had he even
come into the laundromat? she wondered.
If so, where was he now?

Nellie asked a woman who was stuffing
clothes into a dryer whether she had seen a
man putting muddy trousers into one of the
washers. She shook her head.

Nan had no better luck. Another woman
told her she had been too busy to notice
what the others were doing.

Maybe the men could tell us something,
Nan thought, when suddenly Nellie exclaimed, "Look at Freddie!"

The girls turned to see the little boy slip-
ping off his shirt. He quickly dropped it
into one of the washers.

"What are you up to?" Nan asked, running over to him.

"We can't just hang around here without
doing some laundry!" Freddie explained.
"So I'm going to wash my shirt!"

"But what about the money?" Nellie inquired.

Freddie winked and jiggled the coins in

his pocket. "It's my spending money. I earned it."

Sitting in the carrier basket, Flossie looked approvingly at her brother.

"Give me the soap now, Floss," the boy said, and his twin handed him two packets.

"Where'd you get those?" Nan asked.

Freddie pointed to the dispenser. "Over there. Something went flooey and I got two packages instead of one."

"Don't put two in," Nan warned him.

"Why not? It'll make my shirt extra clean."

In spite of Nan's protests, Freddie emptied the packages into the washing machine, closed the door, and pressed the button. A red light blinked on and the shirt began to tumble about.

Freddie, meantime, had spied a beverage machine and pushed the carrier over to it. "Flossie, you like orange or root beer?"

"Orange."

Freddie put a coin in the machine, and *plop,* down dropped a little white cup, which was promptly filled with orange soda. Freddie gave it to his sister.

All at once he heard Nan's voice. "Look what's happening!"

"For goodness sake!" one of the women exclaimed. "What a mess!"

Freddie wheeled about so fast that Flossie nearly fell out of the basket. The orange soda sloshed all over her.

At the sight of his washing machine, Freddie clapped a hand to his forehead. "Oh, no!" he cried.

The door had sprung open, and billows of white suds were pouring out onto the floor. Nan leaped forward and closed the door. With hands on hips she eyed Freddie sternly. "See what you did? You put in too much soap!"

"I'll fix it," Freddie said. He stomped about in the suds until they were reduced to a wet blob. Nellie, meanwhile, found a mop and gave it to him.

Swish—swish. The water disappeared and Freddie said, "See? The floor's even cleaner now."

One of the women chuckled. "Nothing seems to bother that little boy."

Now Nan and Nellie turned their attention to the two men. They were seated on a bench, patiently watching the clothes tumbling in the dryers. The first man could offer no information, but when Nan questioned the second, he said, "Oh, yes. I did see a fellow come in with a pair of pants. I thought it was unusual, because that's all he had."

"What did he do?" Nan asked.

"He put them into the machine down at the end." The man pointed, then added, "He left and hasn't come back yet."

The girls crossed to the machine, followed by Freddie and Flossie. The wash was done, and the limp, damp trousers were lying inside!

·8·

Tower of Pizza

"Now we've got him!" Freddie exclaimed. "As soon as he comes back for the pants—zowie! We'll grab him."

"We'd better call the police and let them do the grabbing," Nellie advised.

Just then, a man wearing a plaid hat came through the door and hurried toward the washer. Nan gasped. It was the same man who had run off with the oats! The girl was so frightened she couldn't speak.

The thief recognized her instantly. He wheeled about and, by the time Nan managed to scream for help, he had raced down the street.

"That's the one! That's the thief!" Nan cried, running outside. Nellie and Flossie raced after her, followed by Freddie.

The thief dashed around the corner. Nan's legs flew and she skidded around the turn just in time to see the man duck into a supermarket. She stopped to let the others catch up.

"He's in that store," she panted excitedly. "We'll all go in quietly and look for him. Whoever sees him first, yell!"

The automatic door swung open and the youngsters walked in. The eight wide aisles were crowded with shoppers pushing their carts. Nan noticed that there was an exit sign in the rear of the store.

The children looked down one aisle after another. Suddenly they spied the man at the far end of the third aisle. He was boxed in by two stout ladies pushing carts piled high with groceries.

"Stop that man!" Nan cried out, and the children raced after him.

Everyone turned to see what the shouting was about. Even the manager came running.

"Here! Here! What's all the noise?" he asked.

"That man!" Nan pointed to the fellow struggling to free himself from between the two carts. "Catch him, he's a thief!"

The fugitive shoved so hard that one of the women staggered backward.

Slam! The cart tipped, throwing the mountain of food to the floor. The man scrambled free and headed for the rear exit. A customer reached out to grab him, but he shook free.

Then the thief ducked past a huge tower of boxes containing pizza mix. A big sign annnounced the merchandise: SPECIAL SALE—TOWER OF PIZZA.

The children struggled forward among the confused customers. Nellie tripped over the scattered groceries, but Nan leaped nimbly aside. She could see the man's plaid hat bobbing this way and that as he raced frantically to get out.

Nellie picked herself up, only to step on

a rolling can of beans. She pitched forward into the Tower of Pizza! The boxes came tumbling down, covering her completely.

"Nellie! Nellie!" Nan called out and turned to help her friend.

In the hubbub, the man leaped over a chain barrier, dashed out the back way, and disappeared.

Nan looked down at Nellie, let out a big sigh, and began to dig into the pile of pizza boxes. Flossie helped her as did the store manager and several customers. Finally they pulled Nellie out.

"I'm—I'm sorry," the girl said tearfully.

"Are you hurt?" asked the manager.

"Some little bumps, that's all," Nellie replied. "I feel all right."

"What did that man steal?" the grocer went on.

"A pony."

"What! Not from my store!" the man stared at them for a moment, then smiled. "Of course, you're fooling."

"No, we aren't," Nan said. "He stole a pony from the riding club."

"I'll inform the police," the manager volunteered. "Too bad," he added. "You nearly had him."

The children nodded glumly.

"We still know where his pants are," Flossie said suddenly. "They might give us a clue!"

"Oh, I forgot all about them!" Nan exclaimed. "That's a wonderful idea, Floss."

"Come on!" Freddie said. "We'd better get them fast!"

The children hurried to the laundromat, and Nan dashed to the washing machine where they had left the pants. *It was empty!*

"Did that man come for his trousers?" Nan asked the other customers.

"Yes," one of the women replied.

"Then why didn't you catch him?" Nellie asked.

Another woman said, "He rushed in and out so quickly that we didn't have a chance."

"Well, come on, Freddie. Get your shirt," Nan said, disappointed.

Her brother took his shirt from the washer and put it in a dryer. As they waited, Nellie said, "Nan, I'm sorry I knocked over those boxes. Maybe you could have caught that man if I hadn't."

Nan put an arm around her friend. "He won't get away forever, Nellie."

A few minutes later, Freddie squirmed into his warm, dry shirt and said, "Let's go home. I'm hungry."

"First, we're going to stop at the television studio," Nan said, "and get an application for the talent show."

Nellie excused herself, saying that she had an errand to run for her mother. Flossie, Freddie, and Nan walked a few more blocks to the tall building where the television station was located. Nan asked the elevator man where they should go, and he told them the tenth floor. The Bobbseys entered an office with a reception desk near the door. It had a plate which read: MISS TINA NIELSEN. The children walked on a rug so soft that they could not hear their footsteps.

"Hello," said the young receptionist.

"We're here for an application," Nan said.

The woman smiled. "For the talent show?"

"Yes. There are four of us and we would like to sing."

"That'll be fine," Miss Nielsen said. She opened a drawer and pulled out a sheet of paper. "Fill it out here."

Nan took a pencil offered to her by the young woman and wrote down the Bobbseys' names and address.

Miss Nielsen looked over the application and smiled. "Would you like to see a broadcast right now?"

"What's going on?" Freddie asked.

"The twelve o'clock news."

"Oh, yes!" Flossie said.

The receptionist opened the door, walked them down a hall, and pointed to a large glass window.

"David Perez is in there."

Nan had often seen David Perez broadcast the midday news. With Freddie and

Flossie at her side, she looked through the window. The newscaster was seated at a desk, facing two television cameras. He was a dark-haired man with a handsome face and a small mustache. Suddenly the girl had a brainstorm and hurried back to the receptionist's desk.

"Oh, Miss Nielsen, Cupcake has been stolen. He's a pony. Maybe Mr. Perez can help us find him!"

The woman quickly wrote something on a piece of paper, then took it down the hall into the studio. She slipped the note to the broadcaster. He glanced at the message, looked through the studio window, and beckoned to Nan.

"Me?" Her lips formed the word, and the announcer nodded vigorously.

Nan's heart thumped as she opened the door and walked into the TV studio.

·9·

The Mysterious Hut

Nan gulped hard, and her knees shook a little, but she made her way to the newscaster's desk.

David Perez reached out to take her hand and drew her to his side. "And now, ladies and gentlemen, we have an unusual request. This is Nan Bobbsey."

Nan looked at the camera with a little red light over the lens. She blinked and smiled.

The newscaster continued, "Nan will tell you her story in her own words." He stood up, slipped the microphone over his neck and put it around hers.

Nan thought, Oh, dear, I wonder if anybody's looking.

Then she coughed, just once, and began. "Cupcake, a Shetland pony, has been stolen. If you find him, or know where he is, please call me, or the Lakeport Police Department."

She described the lost pony and concluded, "If the bad man who stole him is watching this program, please feed Cupcake!"

Nan lifted the mike from her neck and handed it back to David Perez. She thanked him, and the youngsters left the studio.

In the meantime, while waiting for his lunch, Bert tuned in the midday program. When Nan appeared on the TV screen, he looked startled, then shouted, "Mother! Dad! Come quick!" Mr. Bobbsey had just returned from the lumberyard and was chatting with his wife in the kitchen.

"Nan's on TV!" the boy exclaimed. "And she's advertising for Cupcake!"

"I don't know how she managed it," Mrs. Bobbsey said, "but I think she's pretty brave."

"She sure is," Bert agreed. "I'd be tongue-tied."

Ten minutes later, Nan, Flossie, and Freddie ran into the house, their faces glowing.

"We all saw you," said Mrs. Bobbsey, hugging Nan. "You were wonderful!"

"Was it hard?" Bert asked.

"A little scary," Nan replied. Then she told about everything else that had happened.

"All of you were very brave," Mrs. Bobbsey said, "to chase that man through the supermarket."

"You're pretty good detectives," Bert admitted. "But," he added, "you didn't catch the crook!"

"Maybe you can do better," Nan replied.

"We're going to try. Charlie, Freddie, and I are going to take our pup tents and sleeping bags, and spend a night in the pinewoods. That way we can search better."

"When?" Flossie asked.

"Tonight."

The boys spent the rest of the day preparing for their expedition. They packed blankets, extra clothes, cooking utensils, bacon, eggs, and bread.

After dinner, they set off on their bicycles and rode to a place halfway between Lakeport and the state park.

There they dismounted and pushed their bikes a mile into the dense woods. Every step of the way, they looked carefully about, but there was not a sign of anybody.

Finally, they came to a wall of rock about six feet high.

"Let's camp here," Bert suggested. "It's a good, protected spot."

Using stones to hammer in the pegs, the boys pitched their pup tents. As they unrolled their sleeping bags, the wind sighed through the tops of the pine trees and the clouds dropped low.

No sooner had the campers stowed their food safely under the canvas, when fingers of lightning streaked through the dark sky and thunder rumbled in the distance.

"See you all early for breakfast," Bert called to Charlie and Freddie, then closed his tent flap. The others shouted their "good-nights" and soon all were fast asleep.

But suddenly, in the middle of the night, the rain began beating a tattoo against the tents. Bert awoke with a start. As he opened the tent flap, a brilliant flash of lightning was followed by a shattering thunder clap.

Crack! came the noise of splintering

wood, then the deafening crash of a falling tree.

"Wow!" Bert breathed, "that was close!" He looked out again and saw that the other tents were safe. Grinning shakily, he thought, I bet nobody's sleeping!

Freddie was wide awake. He wished he could crawl in with his brother, but was afraid to open the tent flap.

The howling of the wind grew into a steady scream, and one by one the pegs of Freddie's tent pulled loose from the wet ground. Suddenly, the tent was ripped from over him, as if a giant hand had pulled it free. With rain streaming down his face, the little boy ran toward Bert's tent, shouting for help.

Instantly, the older boys crawled out of their tents.

"What'll we do?" Freddie yelled above the roar of the wind.

"Get the tent!" Bert replied.

The three followed the blowing canvas as best they could. Suddenly, it swirled against a tree and they pulled it off. Huddled under the canvas, they sat on a large rock until the wind subsided.

"Come on," Bert said at last. "Let's go back."

They pushed into the blinding rain. Suddenly Charlie called out, "What's that over there?"

"Where?" Bert asked.

"It's a light!" Freddie exclaimed, and pointed toward the woods.

The boys looked through the dripping forest at an eerie glow some hundred yards ahead. Bert led the way toward it. In flickers of lightning, they saw the outline of a small hut. Beside it was a lean-to.

"Somebody's living there," Freddie whispered. "Maybe it's the crook!"

"Follow me quietly," Bert ordered. He dropped to his hands and knees and began to crawl toward the lean-to. A dark shadow moved under the overhanging roof.

Bert crept closer for a better look.

"Hey!" he whispered. "It's Cupcake!"

All at once the light inside the shack went out; a banging sound followed. Frightened, the boys scampered back into the darkness.

"What was that?" Charlie asked.

"Maybe someone heard us and came out to look," Bert guessed.

Silently they watched, but could see nobody, and the light did not reappear.

"Let's untie Cupcake now," Freddie urged.

"No," Bert said. "Someone may be hiding, ready to grab us. We'd better come back at daybreak."

"That's right," Charlie agreed. "Then we can see what we're doing."

The campers retreated into the woods, and finally found their way back to the tents. Freddie crawled in with Bert. They took their wet clothes off, wrapped themselves in dry blankets, and soon fell asleep again.

When Bert awakened, he sat up and looked out. Daylight was just creeping down through the tops of the pine trees. He awakened the others.

"Are you fellows all right?"

"Okay, but my clothes are still soggy," Charlie said ruefully.

The boys dressed and walked cautiously in the direction of the hut. The door stood open.

"There it is!" Bert whispered. "Be careful!" He dropped to his stomach and inched forward to the lean-to. As he elbowed his way around the corner of the hut, he could hardly believe his eyes.

The lean-to was empty!

·10·

The Iron Door

Bert sprang to his feet. Cautiously, he stepped to the window of the hut and peeked in. Empty! He beckoned to the others, who came running.

"We've been tricked!" Bert said. "Cupcake's gone!"

The boys' faces fell. "You mean that guy took him away?" Charlie asked.

"Maybe we can catch them," Freddie suggested. "Come on!"

"It's no use," Charlie said. "The thief probably had a good head start."

Bert nodded. "My guess is he heard us last night and cleared out after the rainstorm."

"Look here," Charlie said, pointing to hoof marks in the soft earth. "Let's see where they lead."

The boys followed the trail till they came to a little clearing among the trees. There the hoof marks ended, only to be replaced by the telltale diamond tire print!

Now on the double, Bert led his two companions through the pinewoods, zigzagging this way and that, till they finally came to the road.

Prints in the ground at the edge of the asphalt showed that the tires had headed in the direction of Lakeport.

"Let's go back," Bert said. "I want to get a better look at that hut!"

The boys trotted through the woods. When they came to the shack, Bert said, "Charlie, suppose you go and start a fire for breakfast, while Freddie and I look around here."

"Okay," Charlie said. "Do you have any waterproof matches?"

Bert reached into his pocket and pulled out a packet, handing it to his friend.

Charlie found dry wood in the lean-to, picked up an armful, and headed for the tents.

Meanwhile, the Bobbsey boys approached the open door of the hut. Bert stepped into the musty room and looked around. Facing him was a crude fireplace made of fieldstones. In front of it was a wooden table and two chairs. Several dirty paper plates lay on the table beside a half-burned candle. Two old cots, covered with newspaper, were the only other items of furniture.

The brothers looked underneath the cots, but found nothing but dust.

Two empty milk cartons under the table bore the name of a local dairy, and the newspapers were also from Lakeport.

"It seems there are two thieves," Freddie declared.

Suddenly Bert spied a square iron door at the side of the chimney. He opened it and peered into the black interior.

"What's in there?" Freddie asked.

"I see something, but I can't make it

out," Bert replied. He put his hand in gingerly, and his fingers touched a smooth object. He pulled it out: *an old saddlebag!*

"Wow!" Bert exclaimed. "This might be the one that was stolen from Wink!"

Freddie quickly looked into the pockets of the saddlebag, but they were empty. "The crooks got the song, too," he said in disgust. "I wonder what they did with it."

Taking the saddlebag with them, the brothers hurried through the woods. Soon they saw white smoke rising slowly in the damp air.

"Umm, I smell something good," Freddie said, and the two ran faster.

At the campfire, Charlie was turning bacon in the skillet. When it was finished, he laid the crisp pieces on three plates and cracked eggs into the sizzling fat.

Using a forked stick, Freddie and Bert toasted bread over the open fire, and soon the boys were enjoying a hearty breakfast. While they ate, Bert told about what they had found in the old hut.

"I think we're closing in on the thieves," Charlie said. "But where's Cupcake? If the crooks drove him back to Lakeport, where would they hide him?"

The boys considered the possibilities: in someone's backyard? in a vacant house? in an empty garage? maybe even on a boat, moored at the dock on the river?

The last idea, suggested by Bert, seemed to be the wildest, and Freddie laughed at the picture of a pony riding in a boat.

"It's not so funny," Charlie said. "That's how Shetlands came to this country in the first place—by boat."

"Come on," Bert said finally. "This isn't catching the crooks."

The boys cleaned their dishes in a nearby puddle of water, doused the fire thoroughly, packed their belongings, and pushed the bicycles through the wet woodland. Then they hopped on and pedaled swiftly over the road, still wet from the storm at night.

"I know where there's a phone booth," Bert said. "We can call police headquarters from there."

The excitement over the discovery banished all thoughts of weariness, and the bike tires made a merry hum on the slick pavement.

Soon they stopped in front of a telephone booth and Bert dismounted to call the police. After he had relayed all the information to the desk sergeant, he said, "We're all going to stop at the riding club and give Wink the saddlebag."

"Okay, thanks, Bert," the sergeant said.

The campers set off again, and pedaled the short distance to the riding club. After

parking their bikes, Bert took the saddlebag, and they all went into the horse barn.
There they found Wink putting a new shoe
on the right rear hoof of Dusk.

"Hello, boys," he said. "What brings you
down here so early?"

"This," Bert said, and thrust the old
saddlebag toward him. Wink let go of the
horse's hoof and stared.

"Well, I'll be a monkey's uncle!" the
stableman exclaimed, reaching for the bag.
"This is mine, all right. Where'd you find
it?"

"In a hut in the woods," Charlie spoke
up.

"But," Bert said, shaking his head, "the
old ballad has been stolen."

"Did you look in the secret compartment?" Wink asked.

"No. You didn't tell us there was one."

"I'll show you," Wink said, "but I need a
knife."

"Let me get the hunting knife from my
knapsack," Charlie said and ran to his bicy-

cle. He returned with a leather sheath and pulled out a shining blade.

Wink took it in one hand, and with the other held a flap of the saddlebag close to his eyes. "There it is," he said, probing for a tiny crack in the leather. Gradually a seam opened, and the stableman slipped his fingers into the compartment. He pulled out a weathered piece of paper on which some music was written.

"Here's your ballad, Bert!" he said with a cheerful grin.

· 11 ·

A Helpful Clue

Bert's bright eyes darted over the music, and he read the lyrics.

"Wink!" he said excitedly. "This is exactly what we need for the TV contest!"

"Come into the office," the stableman invited. "You can try it on my guitar."

The boys hurried to the stable office where Wink's guitar hung from a peg on the wall. Bert strummed a few chords and began to sing the ballad of the lost pony.

Wink stroked his beard and nodded approval. "Now you'll have to start your singing practice and—" He was interrupted by the sound of sirens approaching. Bert put down the guitar and rushed outside with his companions in time to see two police cars driving up to the stables. Chief Smith was at the wheel of the first one.

"Come on, Bert," he called. "We'd like you to take us to the shack in the woods."

Bert looked at his camping mates, but Charlie said, "Go ahead, we'll see you later."

With a wave to Wink, Bert hopped into the back seat behind the chief and a patrolman named Ken Bennett. Sirens wailing, they passed startled drivers heading for the state park. Finally, Bert pointed out the spot where the fugitive's car had left the woods.

Both cruisers slowed down, and Chief Smith, picking his way carefully among the trees, drove into the pinewoods.

"There's the clearing," Bert said.

The chief stopped and the three got out, followed by two policemen in the second car. Soon they reached the hut.

"This place used to belong to Old Man

Dempsey," Officer Bennett said. "He fixed it up for a hunting lodge. He died several years ago and I guess it's been empty since then."

The chief examined the interior, then, opening a kit, took fingerprints from the doorknob, tabletop, and the candle.

"They're quite smudged," he said, disappointed.

"Do you think the crooks will come back here?" asked Bert.

"I doubt it," the chief replied. "But I'll stake it out with two men anyway, just in case."

The officers in the second squad car were ordered to move their vehicle out of sight, then hide among the trees nearby and watch the shack.

The chief and Officer Bennett drove back with Bert, dropping off the boy at the stables so that he could get his bike. Charlie and Freddie were already gone, and on the way home, Bert kept whistling the tune of the old ballad.

He found Freddie and Flossie playing in the backyard. His mother was in the kitchen, covering a big yellow cake with swirls of chocolate icing.

He told of his adventures, and when he came to the part about the ballad, Mrs. Bobbsey put the finished dessert aside and led the way into the living room where she sat down at the piano.

After playing the piece twice, she instructed her children in the harmony. Soon they were practicing their TV contest song.

After an hour, Mrs. Bobbsey glanced at her watch. "Lunchtime!" she announced.

"Good!" Freddie exclaimed. "May we have a piece of that cake?"

"No. I'm taking it to the church food sale this evening," his mother replied. "But I made one just like it for us." She pinched Freddie's cheek. "You don't think I'd forget you, do you?"

That evening after dinner, Mrs. Bobbsey put the cake in a large box and told the twins that she was going to deliver it to the church.

"Bert, Nan, you're in charge. If there's an emergency, call Daddy. He said he had to work late tonight."

Nan nodded and sat down at the piano. The children practiced their song until Flossie yawned and decided to go to bed.

Freddie was about to follow when the telephone rang. Nan picked it up and a man's deep voice came over the line. "Is this Nan Bobbsey?"

"Yes, it is."

"Were you on TV yesterday?"

"Yes, I was," Nan replied. "Do you know anything about Cupcake?"

"Maybe I do, maybe I don't."

"Who are you?"

"My name's Robert Herslow and I'm a truck driver from Allentown."

"What do you know about our pony?"

The man explained that he had been in Lakeport that morning making deliveries in the dock area at the foot of River Street.

"There's an old, deserted garage next to the Acme Warehouse," Mr. Herslow went on. "I heard a thumping noise inside, so I looked in the window and saw a big head, like a dog's or a pony's, maybe."

"What did you do about it?" Nan asked.

"Nothing. In fact, I didn't think anything of it until I was on the road. Then I remembered your broadcast, so I thought I'd call you."

"Thank you so much!" Nan said.

"I might be wrong," Mr. Herslow went on, "so take a look yourself. But be careful." With that, he hung up.

Nan told Bert and Freddie about the conversation, adding, "Wasn't he a nice man to call us?"

"He sure was," Freddie said. "Do you think he really saw Cupcake?"

"We'll have to go and look," Bert decided. "Nan, why don't you stay here with Flossie. If we run into trouble, we'll call Dad."

Nan nodded and the two boys set out on their bicycles. It was not dark yet, but they carried flashlights. Carefully, they passed through the heavier traffic at the center of town and soon turned off onto River Street. On one side were docks, on the other factories and warehouses.

It was dusk when Bert stopped in front of a dark, four-story building with the name ACME WAREHOUSE painted across the second-floor windows.

"This is the place," he said. "The garage must be around back."

The boys steered their bikes down a dark alley until they came to the rear of the building. There they spied a shabby two-car garage.

After parking their bikes in the alley, they walked silently up to the building. Bert stood on tiptoes and peered through a high window. It was so dirty that he could hardly see the interior.

Turning on his flashlight, Bert aimed it inside. He could make out a shaggy animal standing at the back.

He squinted his eyes to see better. There was no doubt. *It was Cupcake!*

The boy flicked off his light and turned to

his brother. "He's in there, all right."

"Let's get him!" Freddie suggested excitedly.

"Maybe there's someone with him," Bert cautioned.

Freddie sucked in his breath. "Then they've seen your light. They'll be coming out after us!"

Bert put his hand on Freddie's arm. "Wait. Don't panic. Let's listen for a while." The brothers put their ears against the side of the garage and stood still. All that could be heard was the noise of Cupcake's hooves, pawing against the cement floor.

Finally Bert stepped toward the door. He opened it a crack. Nothing happened.

"Come on, Freddie," he said, and the two boys stepped over the threshold. They walked forward.

Suddenly, without warning, Bert and Freddie were roughly seized from behind.

"Now we've got you!" said a harsh voice.

·12·

The Rescue

At home, Nan had a strange feeling that all was not well with her brothers. She thought about the mysterious telephone call. Could it have been a hoax by Danny Rugg?

Nan reached for the telephone, then hesitated. "If it's a false alarm and I call the police, everybody will laugh at me. Well, I'll phone Dad, anyway."

She dialed the number of the lumberyard. The watchman's voice answered. "No, your father isn't here now. I don't know when he'll be back."

Disappointed, Nan thanked him and hung up.

I can't leave Flossie, and if I wait for Mother to come back it might be too late, she said to herself. Then she called Nellie and asked her if she could babysit. Nellie agreed and five minutes later arrived breathless at the front door.

"Thanks a lot," Nan said. "And please tell my mother what happened." She rushed out, got on her bicycle, and soon turned into the alley beside the warehouse. She spied the boys' bikes and heard shouts from inside the garage. Then she saw Bert, Freddie, and two men wrestle their way out the side door!

Nan instantly recognized the man grappling with Freddie as the fellow who had made off with the sack of oats—the same one they had nearly caught at the laundromat.

The brothers were fighting like young tigers to escape from the thugs. Bert broke away from his assailant, but the man reached out and grabbed him again. As Bert yelled, the man with the plaid hat picked up Freddie and started to carry him back into the garage where he could not escape.

"Help!" Freddie shouted.

Nan steered her bicycle full tilt toward the man tussling with the little boy.

Crash! The bike banged into the man. His hat flew off as he was knocked flat to the ground. Freddie tumbled, too, but bounced up like a jack-in-the-box. The impact jarred Nan out of her seat. She let her bicycle fall to the ground, then got up and raced to help her brothers.

While Freddie sat on the stunned man, the girl flung herself on the back of the other fellow. "You let my brother go!" she cried, pounding him with her fists.

At that moment, two headlights swept into the alley. A car screeched to a halt. The door flew open and Mr. Bobbsey leaped out.

"Stand back, kids!" he shouted. Nan released her hold on the man. He let go of Bert and turned to run. But one stiff punch from Mr. Bobbsey was all it took to send the fellow sprawling.

"Wow! Dad kayoed him!" Freddie cried out.

Just then, another car crept silently into the alley. From it jumped two policemen, who raced to the scene of the fight. Officer Bennett was one of them.

They collared the thieves and dragged them to their feet.

"What's going on here?" Officer Bennett asked.

"They're the crooks who stole Cupcake—the pony," Bert said. "See for yourself. He's in the garage."

Officer Bennett went in and returned moments later leading Cupcake. He handed the reins to Bert, then said to his colleague, "You handcuff these men, Steve. I'm going back inside. There's something else I want to look at."

Followed by the children, Officer Bennett went into the garage again. He shone a strong light around. Along one wall was something covered with a tarpaulin. He flipped the canvas off: there was the green truck with the diamond tires!

"So this was the thieves' hideout in town!" Bert exclaimed.

"Sure thing," the officer said. "You children have solved a mystery that had us baffled!" He added that the night watchman at the Acme Warehouse had heard the ruckus and had notified headquarters. "But luckily your dad got here ahead of us." He smiled at Mr. Bobbsey, who gingerly rubbed the knuckles of his right hand.

"Your mother called me," Mr. Bobbsey said to the children. "She got home shortly after Nan left."

"What about Cupcake?" Nan asked as Officer Bennett herded the two prisoners into the patrol car. "May we keep him tonight?"

The police and Mr. Bobbsey consented. After promising to call Mr. Rockwell, the officers drove off.

With Bert and Freddie pushing their bikes, and Mr. Bobbsey driving slowly behind them, Nan rode Cupcake home. Mrs. Bobbsey found a comfortable place for the pony in the garage, before begging to hear every detail of the adventure.

Eyes sparkling, the children told their mother about the capture of the thieves. By the time they had finished, the telephone rang. Bert jumped up to grab it.

It was Chief Smith. He reported that the two criminals had confessed! They had stolen Cupcake to sell him to a circus, but the young detectives had kept them on the run so that they had found no chance to make the sale.

"They had sneaked in earlier to spy on the stables," Chief Smith explained. "That's when they took the saddlebag, hoping to sell it for an antique."

The men also admitted stealing the horses from the Chatham academy. They had been sold to an out-of-state stable, but would soon be returned to their rightful owner.

When Flossie awakened next morning, Nan led her in her nightgown downstairs to the garage.

"Oh, Cupcake's back!" Flossie cried, hugging him again and again.

The excitement lasted all day, especially

when the newspapers carried big headlines about the capture of the animal thieves and praised the Bobbseys for their part in the arrests.

Even Danny Rugg tried to be friendly, but the young heroes were too busy practicing for the TV contest to pay much attention to him. With Bert strumming his guitar, the children sang their ballad over and over.

"That's fine," their mother said as she listened to the sweet harmony. "I think you might really have a chance to win."

By supper Friday night, the youngsters were nervous. Half an hour before showtime Nan was shivering.

"I have butterflies in my tummy," she said.

Flossie looked surprised. "Will they fly out when you sing?"

The others laughed and that made them feel better. Their parents drove them to the TV station, where they took the elevator to the studio.

"We have eight acts scheduled," Miss

Nielsen said as they entered the office. "You're going to be third, and your friend David Perez is the emcee."

The first act was a brother-and-sister dance team. The Bobbseys watched with the other contestants on a monitor set in the reception room and heard the audience clap loudly.

Next came a boy trumpet player. He was very good, too.

"How will the winner be chosen, Miss Nielsen?" Nan asked.

This would be decided, they were told, by a sound meter, which would register the applause of the audience.

Next came the Bobbseys' turn. They walked on the stage with the lights shining in their faces and two television cameras in front of them.

Bert ran his fingers over the strings of his guitar. They they sang their ballad while the audience listened in silence. When the song was over, a thunder of clapping filled the studio. Loudest of all was a man named

Cobb Winkler, who sat in the last row.

Bert led his brother and sisters back into the waiting room. It seemed to take a long time for the other five acts to finish. Two of them, a girl roller skater and a harmonica duet, drew loud applause. Freddie looked gloomy. "The harmonicas sound great," he whispered.

Finally, the announcer read the scores on the sound meter. The Bobbseys waited nervously.

"And now for the winner," the dark-haired emcee said, "It is—the Bobbsey twins!"

The children laughed and clapped, and Freddie did a cartwheel. Then they were ushered back into the studio and stood in the center of the stage, surrounded by the other smiling contestants.

"Here is the surprise award for the winners," said David Perez. He gave an envelope to Nan. She opened it and read:

"A trip to California for the whole family! Anytime within the next year."

But more than fun awaited the Bobbseys, because an exciting mystery was to come their way in the adventure called *The Rose Parade® Mystery*.

"I can't wait!" cried Freddie.

"Oh, I'm so happy!" Flossie chirped.